Freddie

Honey

CAN YOU BE AN ARTIST?

Bae

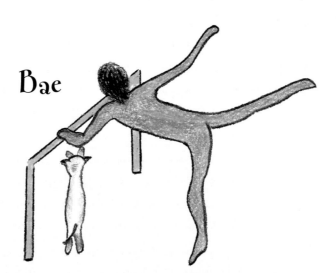

WRITTEN AND ILLUSTRATED BY

LIESEL SOLEY

Book Publishers Network
P. O. Box 2256
Bothell, WA 98041
425-483-3040
www.bookpublishersnetwork.com

10 9 8 7 6 5 4 3 2 1

LCCN: 2010916711
ISBN 13: 978-1-935359-69-2
ISBN 10: 1-935359-69-X

ACKNOWLEDGMENT

Special thanks to Richard Carter for the consistent expertise and integrity he brings to his profession as photographer and designer. Also for the many hours of help in putting together my artistic works, CDs and books.

DEDICATION

For my wonderful and energetic grandnieces and grandnephew

Sophia

Abagail

Hanna

Elena

Angelina

Sterling

Charlotte

Nicole

Addie

Grace

AUTHOR'S NOTE

It is true that Freddie, Honey, and Bae become professional artists. As spiritual beings we are all capable of being beautiful artists, whether we make a living at it or not. There are limitless ways one can create. One can be an artist of life or raising a family or arranging a room. If one truly creates beauty and quality in what one does and if this translates to others, then one is actively being an artist. I sincerely believe this.

— *Liesel Soley*

Hi. I am Freddie.
In my room is the old beaten-up
record player Grandpa gave me.

I also have a fancy CD player.
I listen to music many hours a day.

My mom bakes cakes and
cookies for the church fair.
Something surprising
always happens!

3

My dad is a pilot. I love the cards he sends me, but I wish he was home more. I always know when he is coming home.

My mom gets really busy cooking extra yummy desserts, and I hear her singing a lot.

She gets up very early the day he comes home and fusses around the house making sure everything is spic and span, and fresh flowers are placed in every room.

Then she surprises
me with the news he
will be home that
very day.

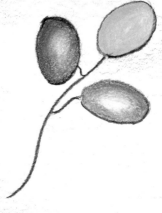

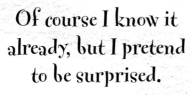

Of course I know it
already, but I pretend
to be surprised.

We are very happy
and excited driving
to the airport.

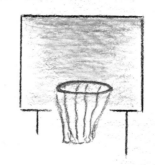

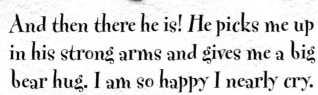
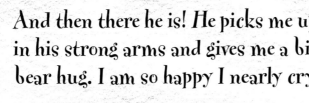

And then there he is! He picks me up
in his strong arms and gives me a big
bear hug. I am so happy I nearly cry.

Everyday I go to the bottom
of the hill to get the mail.

Peter, the mailman, makes me laugh. He whistles and
sings and tells me jokes and sometimes a funny story.

Peter likes music too. He gave me a CD for
my birthday. Peter is my best friend.

My name is Honey. Mark and Steve are my brothers, and I have two sisters, Kate and Cheryl. I am the youngest. My mom decorates other people's houses.

I am supposed to keep my room nice and tidy. I love the pretty flowers she brings in from the garden. All those beautiful colors make my room come alive.

We have lots of flowers and trees in my yard. We also have a great swing and a big slide, and the kids from next door love to come over to play.

My daddy is great. He is a doctor and very busy, but every week he takes us to a show or museum. My favorite is the art museum. The paintings are so different, but each painting seems to have something special to say. The time always goes by too fast, and we have to leave.

Sometimes in the winter my dad takes us skating.
That is always exciting and lots of fun.

Barney, from next door, is one year older than I am, and he likes to show me all sorts of insects and bugs.

He also knows everything about birds and animals. We love to explore the woods and the stream nearby.

I particularly like to be outside in the fall.
I love the colors – oranges and blues and
greens and yellows and reds.

The flowers and trees
and sky seem so happy
to be alive.

They, along with Barney,
are my special friends.

13

I am Bae Cho from Korea. In my village we were all so happy and had such fun. Sometimes when there was a birthday or a wedding and always for Christmas, we would dance and dance and swirl around all night.

My family grew wheat
and rice. We had pigs,
geese, and horses and
other animals.

Now we live in New York City. There are so many things to do here, and I am always discovering something new, especially in Central Park.

My parents own an organic food market on the corner of 75th Street and Broadway. The market is big with all sorts of wonderful foods. It is always full of people. People who are there for the first time are always very excited. My parents have been talking about buying a bigger place. Sometimes they ask me to help out on Saturdays when they get extra busy.

I study a lot and also help other kids with their homework. I save up the money I make, and whenever I can, I go to watch people dance

I get very excited when I see the dancers
and want to run up on stage and join them.
It makes me feel so happy.

When I am there it is like being
in another world.

Freddie, Honey, and Bae don't know each other but in some ways are very much alike.

They daydream a lot, and the three of them are always getting into trouble because their attention is not on what they are doing.

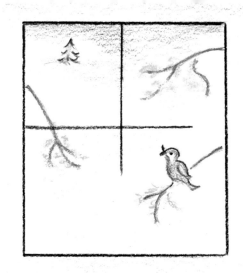

Freddie daydreams about playing the violin instead of paying attention to his teacher, Mr. Snorky. He gets very rattled.

When Honey daydreams about painting, she drops things and makes a lot of messes. She drives her mom bananas.

Bae is always tripping over himself when he is daydreaming about dancing. He is so clumsy. Even when he visits his aunt who has a big house, he can't seem to remain upright! His aunt gets annoyed every single time.

Yes – the three of them are constantly getting into trouble.

Never mind. Freddie, Honey, and Bae are going in the right direction. All three imagine themselves as artists and now are also sure their wonderful dreams can come true.

Freddie, Honey, and Bae decide to do something about it.

ARTISTS CORNER

24

Freddie sees himself playing in a string quartet and starts practicing his violin regularly. Honey sees her paintings in homes her mom decorates. She experiments with colored pencils and oil paints. And Bae can't wait to dance in his home country. He starts dance classes - tap, jazz, folk, hip-hop, and ballet. Ballet is his favorite.

The three work hard at what they love to do, and guess what?!

Freddie is at the top of his class! Honey's mom is no longer going bananas. And Bae's family is amazed at how strong and skilled he has become. They enjoy success and their families are filled with joy and bursting with pride.

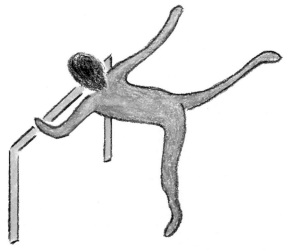

MOZART QUARTET

SOLD

THE MASTER BALLET from AMERICA Sept 3

Can YOU be an artist?

Of course you can! Just unlock your own secret and special world and then

DARE TO FOLLOW YOUR DREAMS!

DARE TO BE YOURSELF!

DARE TO BE FREE!!

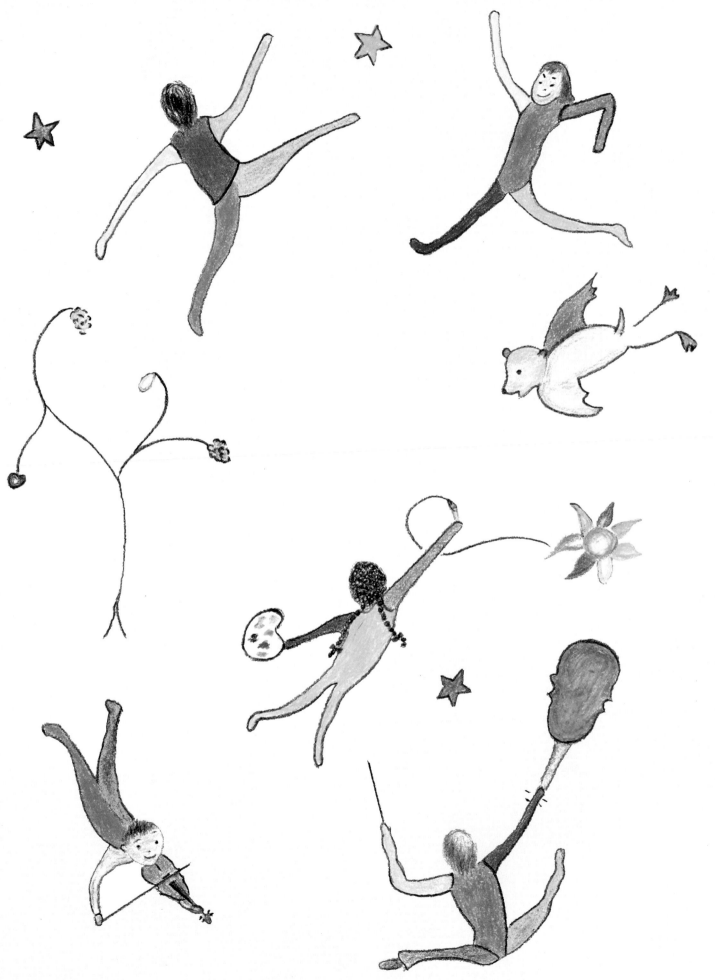

Liesel Soley is a professional violinist. She earned her B.S. and M.S. degrees from Juilliard and was a Fulbright Scholar in Paris, France. Ms. Soley has performed solo recitals in the U.S. and France and is the violinist in the piano trio, "Trio Viva." She has taught violin at the Manhattan School of Music and School of the Arts in New York City, and has taught violin and viola at St. Petersburg College and the Pinellas County Center for the Arts in St. Petersburg, Florida. Ms. Soley is presently teaching violin, viola, and chamber music privately. As an artist she has enjoyed expressing herself through writing, painting, and drawing as well as through music.

lieselsoley@mac.com
http://web.mac.com/lieselsoley

"Liesel is one of those engaging and dedicated musicians that encompasses some of the following words: 'trouper,' 'dynamic,' 'energetic,' and 'spontaneous.' I think her nickname should be 'Vivace,' as that relates to vitality and vividity. The absence of egotism, so evident in her teaching success, is a sterling quality. Like the 'silver ladies' on my vintage Rolls-Royce, she heads off on a chase to a musical horizon with power and grace. Can I say more?

"Her paintings translate and relate to her love of music, for there is movement, meter and 'parts' as in a sonata. There are contrasts and unity and a mathematical playfulness that parallels her musical verve."

— **PETER STILTON**, Fine Artist and Art Educator

"This book feels so close to the heart. Through its warm, lively illustrations, it takes the reader to that place where family is close at hand and it's safe to explore the world of possibility. Once in that space, the text takes over and coaxes the reader's spirit to dance."

— **DAVID J. LANE**, Youth Librarian, Clearwater Public Library System